THE
STORY
BEHIND
SANTA
SACKS

Story by Brian L. Moore

Pictures by Todd Mulligan

Hills-n-Hollows Publishing
St. Marys, Ontario

National Library of Canada Cataloguing in Publication

Moore, Brian L., 1951-
  The story behind Santa sacks / Brian L. Moore ; illustrator, Todd
Mulligan.

ISBN 0-9732651-0-8

I. Mulligan, Todd, 1959- II. Title

PS8576.O5777S86 2003   jC813'.6   C2003-901212-3
PZ7

Distributed by:
Hills-n-Hollows Publishing
Box 1214
St. Marys, Ontario
N4X 1B8
hills-n-hollows@rogers.com

Printed and bound in Canada by Friesens, Altona, Manitoba.

For Gail, Lyle and Douglas.
                    —B.L.M.
For Bonnie, Melinda and Neil.
                    —T.M.

Dear Santa,

Last Christmas you gave me a present that was in a small cloth sack. It made me feel special.

I am going to use it again this year to send a gift to Grandpa. It will make him feel special too.

Santa, is there a story behind the sack? Will I ever get another one?

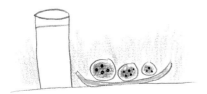

Your friend,

Riley

Dear Riley,

Thank you for your letter. You asked if there was a story behind the cloth sack. There sure is a story, Riley.

These Santa Sacks are very special. Maybe you will get another one from me or from a friend who is passing it on, like you are with your grandfather.

Here is the story, Riley! It's about a cow who wanted fame, some sheep who needed to feel useful and a young elf who went looking to solve a problem at the North Pole.

Your jolly friend,

Santa

P.S. Thanks for the milk and cookies.

It was late November at the North Pole. The elves were almost finished building and boxing the toys that Santa would deliver to the girls and boys that year.

Santa stared at the pile of boxes.

"Oh, my!" he exclaimed. "There are more boxes every year!"

"That's because there are more good little girls and boys every year," said Gail. Gail was Santa's elf in charge of wrapping Christmas presents. "I wonder if we will have enough wrapping paper for all of these," she added.

Santa adjusted his spectacles and checked his list twice. "You're right, Gail! There *are* more names," he announced. "Please have your sons check my tree farm to see if I have enough trees to make all the wrapping paper that we need this year."

The moon shone brightly as Gail's two sons, Lylo and Doogy, hiked through the crunchy snow to Santa's tree farm. Lylo's voice echoed in the still air. "These are the trees that I use to make wrapping paper."

"You make wrapping paper from trees?" asked Doogy.

"That's right. There are 30 groups of trees. Each year we use one group and then we plant seeds so that in 30 years we'll have trees we can use again. The problem is that our groups of trees are too small to produce enough paper for all the boxes!"

"Let's go chop down some more trees," said Doogy innocently.

"That wouldn't be right," replied Lylo. "If we did that, we would be using next year's trees."

"We sure do have a problem here," moaned Doogy sadly.

"We must tell Mom and Santa!" Lylo exclaimed.

Gail and her two sons told Santa the sad news.
There would not be enough wrapping paper for
Santa's gifts.

Santa frowned. "I can't use any more trees. What will I do?"

Santa, Gail and Lylo sat down to think.

Doogy walked sadly to the barn to visit his friend Moocandoo, the cow.

Moocandoo had lived at the North Pole for many years, but only Doogy and Santa believed that she was more than just an ordinary cow. In a warm stall at the back of the barn, Doogy found his friend Moocandoo—the cow who had jumped over the moon.

"Why the tear, Doogy Boy?" asked Moocandoo.

Doogy explained everything. "We don't have enough wrapping paper for Santa's gifts! I need to find an idea. I need your help, Moocandoo!"

They heard giggles from the reindeer stalls.

"Moocandoo can help!" Doogy yelled. "Why don't you all believe that?"

"Easy there, Doogy Boy," Moocandoo whispered softly. "You have to prove yourself useful or the reindeer tease. Their laughing doesn't bother me."

Doogy pleaded, "Use your power, Moocandoo! Help Santa and prove to the reindeer that you are useful. Help me find an idea!"

"I wish I could help," sighed Moocandoo. "I know the pain of wanting something and not being able to find it."

"What did you want that you couldn't find?" asked Doogy as he gently stroked the soft face of Moocandoo.

For the first time Moocandoo told her story, because she knew that her friend Doogy would listen and believe. "The thing I wanted was fame, Doogy Boy. I had one special power and that was the power to jump. I was going to jump over the moon and become world-famous. I was not going to keep my power secret like my mother had done with hers."

"What was her power?" Doogy wondered aloud.

"She could put big space in a little place. She used her power twice. When her loving but foolish owner sold her for some ordinary beans, she packed enough beanstalk into them to make him rich and famous. It was all because of her that he was able to climb to a giant's house in the clouds and get the giant's share of riches and fame.

"I wanted that kind of fame even if my mother didn't. When she couldn't talk me out of my plan to jump over the moon, Mother used her power one more time. She took an ordinary sack and gave it enough space for food to last me months. It's the same sack that Santa now treasures because it holds thousands of gifts."

"Tell me about your jump, Moocandoo," Doogy insisted.

"My jump was seen by a reporter who only wrote one line: 'The cow jumped over the moon.' He didn't even use my real name. I did not become famous.

"I knew I was a good jumper, but was I any good at landing?

"I went over the moon and headed back to Earth. The land beneath me got closer and closer. As I prepared to crash, it became whiter and whiter. Snow! I landed on the slope of a snowy hill and slid in a straight line all the way to the North Pole, with my sack scattering a long trail of food.

"I stopped beside this barn. Santa came running when he heard his little dog, Jake, laughing at me. I guess I was such a sight. Santa gave me this warm stall and in return I gave him the special sack. I did not get the fame I wanted, Doogy, but I am happy to be alive and with my friends."

"That explains Santa's sack," said Doogy.
"It's a little place with a big space."

"Moocandoo! You saved us, and we didn't know it until now!" cried Chantel, who was one of a dozen fluffy sheep who lived in a cozy pen beside Moocandoo.

Now even the reindeer were listening. "Go ahead, Chantel! Tell us how Moocandoo saved you," they all asked.

Chantel spoke. "We once belonged to a little girl. As time passed, she paid less and less attention to us. We thought she would miss us and look for us if we ran away. She did not even try to find us. Everybody told her, 'Leave them alone and they'll come home.' Well, we did not come home.

"We wandered north, thinking that nobody needed us. Our wool grew long and thick so that we didn't feel the cold. As we travelled, the grass gave way to snow. We would have starved if not for Moocandoo. We ate well as we followed her sliding trail of food all the way to the North Pole.

"Here we are today in a loving home thanks to Moocandoo. You did save us, Moocandoo. Thank you so much! We will never forget you, and that makes you famous, just like you wanted to be. I just wish there was more need for wool here. Most children want toys, not clothes. We've got this huge pile of extra wool and no idea how to use it. Moocandoo has found her fame—I wish we sheep could find a way to be useful."

Doogy's eyes lit up as he had his biggest idea ever. "Thank you! Thank you! Thank you!" he screamed. "Thank you, Moocandoo and Chantel. I've got to run!"

"Thanks for what?" Moocandoo wondered.

"What is it, Doogy?" asked Chantel.

"I'll show you tomorrow!" Doogy replied as he raced for Santa's workshop.

The next morning Santa awoke and was amazed to see Gail with Doogy and Lylo, each boy holding a cute little sack decorated in Christmas colours.

"Ho Ho Ho! You have solved my problem!" he rejoiced. "I can give gifts in little SANTA SACKS. I won't have to cut extra trees."

Gail added, "I can still wrap *some* gifts."

"These sacks will save some trees, and they can be used again and again," Lylo declared.

"Who do I thank for this marvellous idea?" Santa cried happily.

"It was my idea!" cheered Doogy. "I knew we needed a way to wrap gifts without using paper. Moocandoo told me the story of your Santa Sack. Chantel, the sheep, told me about the extra wool. I took the wool to your sewing elves, who were not busy at all, and asked them to make little Santa Sacks out of it."

Santa was very, very pleased.

Everyone at the North Pole heard the wonderful news.

Santa organized a big party. The happy guests of honour were Doogy, Moocandoo and the sheep, who now felt very useful.

Something had been added to the Christmas tradition.

Children still rush to their presents on Christmas morning full of love and joy. They still hope for something special from Santa, and now they know there is a chance that they will receive a Santa Sack.

Now Riley, my little friend, you have learned "The Story Behind Santa Sacks."

Keep asking questions and learning all that you can, because your brain is like Santa's sack: it's a little place, but there is no limit to how much it can hold.

From all of us at the North Pole,
MERRY CHRISTMAS!

Your jolly friend … *Santa*